The Ant Hill
DISASTER

published by

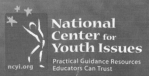

National Center for Youth Issues

Practical Guidance Resources
Educators Can Trust

ncyi.org

www.ncyi.org

For the hole in all of our hearts. – Julia

Foreword

On the evening of December 14, 2012, my husband and I were faced with the unimaginable task of telling our older daughters of our family's loss. Our precious daughter and their little sister, Josephine, had perished in the tragedy at her school, Sandy Hook Elementary.

Though a mother and former elementary school teacher, I grasped for words that could explain the events of that morning... but there were no words.

What I did manage to say was that I knew our Joey was in heaven and we would find a way to carry on together. That we loved them, and so did she, that we would never allow her sparkling personality and loving spirit to be lost in this tragedy.

We came together with family, friends, neighbors, and our community to defy this tragedy with our love.

In the weeks following, we sent our daughters back to school, confident in the love and support they would receive in our community. I volunteered to stay. I wanted to deliver a message: that we were meant to carry on together. And so we began our journey.

Julia Cook's *Ant Hill Disaster* honors this journey out of loss and into hope. She lights the path for the youngest of readers with words, colors, and a familiar setting that young children understand and need. Her adorable characters model team work, empathy, and compassion in a child-friendly story that may translate to a tragic event in their own community or another, man-made or natural.

Ant Hill Disaster is a message of hope and love that will touch and inspire young children and the adults who love them.

Michele Gay
Mother of Josephine Gay
Co-Founder of Safe and Sound: A Sandy Hook Initiative

Duplication and Copyright

National Center for Youth Issues
ncyi.org
Practical Guidance Resources
Educators Can Trust

P.O. Box 22185
Chattanooga, TN 37422-2185
423.899.5714 • 866.318.6294
fax: 423.899.4547 • www.ncyi.org

ISBN: 978-1-937870-27-0
© 2014 National Center for Youth Issues, Chattanooga, TN
All rights reserved.
Written by: Julia Cook
Illustrations by: Michelle Hazelwood Hyde
Design by: Phillip W. Rodgers
Contributing Editor: Beth Spencer Rabon
Published by National Center for Youth Issues • Softcover
Printed at Starkey Printing, Chattanooga, Tennessee, U.S.A., June 2016

It's almost time for school,
but I don't want to go.

I'm afraid.

I go to the school
up on the hill.

It's for ants.

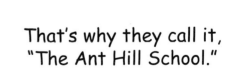

That's why they call it,
"The Ant Hill School."

3

But now it's ruined.

A few weeks ago, a human wearing waffle stomper boots stomped all over the Ant Hill School until he made it flat. It was a disaster!

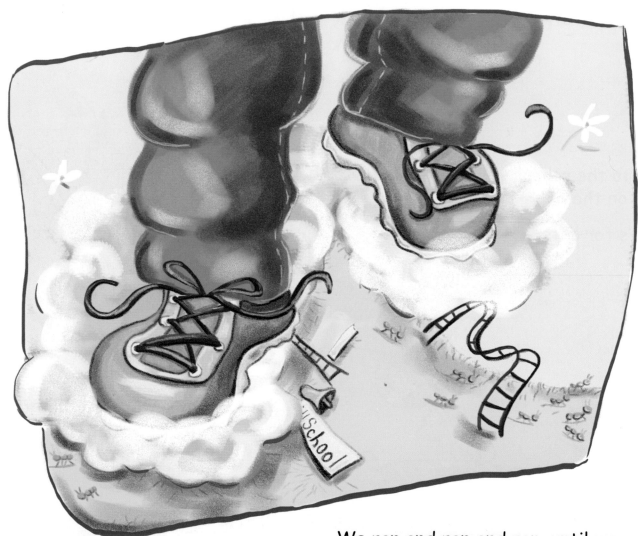

We ran and ran and ran, until we got to the great big tree that's two blocks away, and then we stopped.

Now everything has changed.

"Why did he do it, Mama?" I asked.

"I don't know why," she said.

"Things happen that we have no control over. But we have to find a way to keep living. We have to move forward."

"How do we do that?"

"We breathe in and breathe out, and hold onto each other.
We shed a lot of tears, and we love one another.

We all come together as a strong team of **ONE**, and then we rebuild, and get things done!

"I just can't go today, Mama. I'm too scared!"

"I know how you feel. I'm scared too. But you are safe now, and you need to go."

After school, I will be right outside the door waiting for you, just like always. Then, we can spend some special time together, just you and me! Maybe we can even go to the park!"

"What if it happens again?" I asked.

"Everyone is working together very hard to keep that from happening. We are STRONG when we all work together."

"How strong?"

"VERY, VERY STRONG!"

"When I was about your age, we had a terrible storm. It rained and rained and rained. The sky got very dark and angry. The wind blew so hard that it sounded like a freight train!

Big buildings blew right over. Some of the buildings even blew away!

A big piece of cement landed right on top of our beautiful ant hill and smashed it flat.

It was a DISASTER!"

"What did you do?"

"We took cover until the storm was over. Then, we ran and ran and ran, until we got to the great big tree that's two blocks away, and then we stopped."

9

Then,

"We breathed in and breathed out, and held onto each other.

We shed a lot of tears, and we loved one another.

We all came together as a strong team of **ONE**,

and then we rebuilt, and got things done!

"Were you scared?"

"I was REALLY scared."

"Why did it happen?"

"I don't know why. Things happen that we have no control over.

But, I couldn't stop being who I am.

I had to keep living and growing...and so do you!

So today, you need to go back to school."

When I got to school, things were different.

I saw lots of **sad** faces.

I saw lots of **scared** faces.

I even saw a few **angry** faces.

There were new faces that I had never seen before...and some faces weren't there.

Nobody had a **normal** face.

The worker ants had worked double shifts and built us a brand new school.
But it wasn't as big as our old school...

It wasn't the same...

Nothing was the same.

My teacher hugged each one of us.

She hugged me so tight
that I couldn't even breathe!

Then, with tears in
her eyes she said:

"The world as we know it
has really changed,
and everyone knows
that nothing's the same.

But I'm here for each
and every one of you.

Together, I know that
we can pull through."

"You may feel scared or guilty or sad.

You may feel empty or anxious or mad.

There isn't a right or wrong way to feel.

What happened to us is painful and real."

"But now it's the time
for us to be here.

You're safe right now, so
take charge of your fear!

You have to continue
to learn and grow.

So we'll deal with these changes
together, you know."

"When we work together,
we're a very strong team!

We can get through anything
no matter how bad it seems.

If you need to ask questions,
just know I am here.

I'll give you a hug
and a tissue for tears."

"Our days ahead are going to be rough.

At home and at school, things will be tough.

But we have each other, so take a deep breath.

When we're all here together, you don't need to be stressed."

So that's what we did. We took a deep breath and we started over.

I made it through the day, and
my mom was right where she said
she'd be waiting for me after
school. On the way home, we
even went to the park.

"How was your day?" my mom asked.

"It was OK." I said.

"Do you want to talk about it?"

"NOPE!"

Before I went to bed, I started feeling scared again.

"I don't want to go to school tomorrow, Mama.
I just want to stay home."

"I know how you feel, but you are safe now and you need to
go. After school, I will be right outside the door waiting for
you, just like always. Then, we can spend some special time
together, just you and me! Maybe we can even go back to
the park!"

"What if it happens again, Mama?"

"Everyone is working together very hard to keep that
from happening."

"We are STRONG when
we all work together."

"How strong?"

"VERY, VERY STRONG!"

"Our teacher told us about what happened when you were little today... when the bad storm blew the big piece of cement on top of the hill and smashed it flat."

"What did she say?"

"She said it was a terrible disaster that changed the lives of many ants."

"Then, she said that sometimes, things happen that we have no control over, but we have to find a way to keep living. She told us that what you did is now what we need to do.

"We need to:

Breathe in and breathe out, and hold onto each other.

It's OK to shed tears, but we must love one another.

If we all come together as a strong team of ONE,

then we can rebuild, and get anything done!"

23

"Did she say anything else?"

"No, but she told us that if we wanted to talk about it or ask her questions we could."

"Then, we got to make special cards for all of the ants out there who are sadder than we are."

"Mama...do you think the stomper will come back?"

"Nobody knows the answer to that question, Son, but you know that EVERYONE is working together very hard to keep that from EVER happening again!

And together we are STRONG!"

"How strong?"

"VERY, VERY STRONG!"

"Now go to sleep."

25

Today, going to school was a little bit easier.

Today, going to school was
easier than yesterday.

Today, going to school didn't seem quite as hard.

Today going to school almost felt normal.
Maybe that's because different is now what seems like the same.

"We breathe in and breathe out, we hold onto each other.
We shed a lot of tears, and we love one another.
We've all come together as a strong team of **ONE**.
We've rebuilt our lives, and we're getting things done!

They say that when change happens,
it makes everyone grow.
Our pain is never forgotten, this we all know.
But together we somehow are learning to cope,
because disasters will <u>NEVER</u> take away our hope!

Helping Kids Cope with Disasters and Violence

By Julia Cook

When disasters, both natural and man-caused occur, parents are faced with the challenge of discussing tragic events with their children. Although these might be difficult conversations, they are important and necessary. Always remember, there is no "right" or "wrong" way to talk to your child about traumatic events. However, here are a few tips that you might find helpful:

- Remain calm and reassuring – create an environment where children will feel comfortable asking questions.

- Always answer a child's questions truthfully with simple answers. You don't need to go into more detail than necessary, but lying to your children or making up facts will ultimately confuse them. Eventually, when they find out the truth about what happened, they may struggle with trusting you in the future.

- You may be asked to repeat your answers several times. Be consistent in your reply, and realize that your repetitive answers are reassuring your child's "need to know" and building upon their sense of security.

- Children often feel out of control when disasters occur. Keeping with a familiar routine is very important when trying to reestablish the security of feeling in control.

- If your child asks a question that you do not know the answer to, it's ok to say, "I don't know."

- Acknowledge and normalize your child's thoughts, feelings and reactions. Help children understand why they feel this way.

- Encourage kids to talk about disaster related events on their terms. Never force a child to ask a question or to talk about an incident until he/she is ready.

- Reassure your child that many people out there are helping those who are hurting. You may want to let your child make a card for someone who is suffering. Giving to those in need of support allows a child to feel like he/she can make a difference in helping with a terrible situation.

- Keep your child away from watching news stations and listening to radio where the disaster is being discussed and replayed. Sensationalizing the events that have occurred will only upset and confuse your child further.

- Promote positive coping and problem solving skills. Remember – **You are your child's coping instructor.** Your children take note of how you respond to local and national events. They also may be listening to every word you say when you discuss these events with other adults.

- Emphasize children's resiliency. Fortunately, most children, even those who are exposed to trauma, are quite resilient.

- Children who are preoccupied with questions and concerns about safety should be evaluated by a trained mental health professional. If your child suffers from sleep disturbances, anxiety, recurring fears about death, or severe separation anxiety from parents, contact your school counselor and/or pediatrician.

- Strengthen friendship and peer support, and foster supportive relationships–There is strength in numbers!

- Take care of your own needs. In order to be there for others, you have to take care of yourself.

- Advanced preparation and immediate response will help with healing and coping. All schools have safety plans in place that are continually being evaluated and updated. **Explain to your child that this is a good thing.**

Always Remember: You are your child's coping instructor!